Brilliant

For Ben, Emily and Katy – SH

First published in Great Britain in 2007
by Andersen Press Limited, 20 Vauxhall Bridge Road, London SW1V 2SA
www.andersenpress.co.uk
www.carolineglicksman.com
Reprinted 2007

Text © Simon Hutton, 2007
Illustration © Caroline Glicksman, 2007

British Library Cataloguing in Publication Data available.

ISBN 978 184 270 569 8

Printed in the UK by CPI Bookmarque, Croydon, CR0 4TD

Brilliant Billy's BIG Book of Dinosaurs

Simon Hutton

ANDERSEN PRESS

Chapter One

Billy was brilliant at dinosaurs – just like he was brilliant at everything. And for once, he wasn't the only one saying it.

'Billy certainly knows his dinosaurs,' Mum said wearily to the other mums at the school gate. 'It's dinosaurs day and night.'

And Dad joked, 'Billy's mad. Mad about dinosaurs!'

But it was Billy's teacher, Miss Plum, who really said it. 'Billy's quite the expert at dinosaurs. I think *he* should be the teacher!'

Billy thought that was a brilliant idea! It could have been one of *his*

ideas, it was so brilliant!

Professor Billy, world expert and famous dinosaur teacher ... What a great ring that had to it! So nice, so neat, so *natural.*

He would be a world-famous dinosaur teacher. And since Mum was so interested in dinosaurs, she could be his first lucky pupil. It was the perfect plan.

But Billy was soon to learn that perfect plans don't always go perfectly. Mum was impossible. Oh, she *said* she wanted to learn – but she just wouldn't stay still! It was busy this, busy that. Busy at everything except listening. Billy couldn't catch her, let alone teach her! He realised if he was going to get Mum smarter, he'd have to get smarter himself.

So, early one morning, he crept into Mum's bedroom, clutching two toy dinosaurs.

Dad was at work. Mum was fast asleep, snoring like a drain.

Billy prodded her.

She sniffled and snuffled awake. 'Billy, do you know what the time is!'

Of course he knew what the time was! He was brilliant at telling the time. Billy was brilliant at everything (at least according to Billy).

'The big hand is on the seven and the small hand is . . .'

'Don't tell me!' groaned Mum, rolling over and burying herself in the

7

covers.

Mum was going to be an awkward pupil, Billy could tell. He decided he would wait. He was brilliant at waiting.

Eventually the covers curled back. Mum peeped out.

'Billy, why don't you go back to bed?'

'I've got something to show you.'

'Why don't you show me later?' came the sleepy reply.

'I can't. It's too important.'

Billy held up the first dinosaur. It was a fierce-looking *tyrannosaurus rex*.

'This is a predator,' he said, beginning the lesson.

'*What's* a predator?' asked Mum, squinting at the object in Billy's hand. Without her glasses on, everything was a blur.

'A predator is an animal that eats other animals,' said Billy.

'I know what a predator is. I mean, what's that in your hand? Is it a mouse? Has the cat been bringing in mice again?'

'Mice aren't predators,' said Billy – even though he wasn't sure what a mouse ate. 'Mice are herbivores, like this.' Billy whipped out the second dinosaur and dangled it right in front of Mum's face.

'Yeek!' Mum scrambled up the bed, dragging the covers into a pile around her. 'Get it out of the house! You're worse than the cat!'

Mum was going to burst a blood vessel if Billy didn't do something. He grabbed Mum's glasses and made her put them on.

Mum stopped screaming. She peered at the object in Billy's hand.

'It's *not* a mouse,' she said, like that was something truly amazing.

'It's a stegosaurus,' said Billy.

'A stego-what?'

'It's a *dinosaur*,' sighed Billy.

'Not a real one, I hope.'

'Mu-um! There aren't any dinosaurs alive today. Dinosaurs were much earlier than people.'

'Not as early as some people,' Mum groaned, glancing at the clock by her bed. 'Why don't you go back to sleep?'

'But I want to tell you about dinosaurs.'

'Why don't you tell me later?'

'You'll be busy later. You're always busy. And anyway, you *said* you wanted to know about dinosaurs!'

'I did?'

Billy nodded. 'The other night. You said, "The Jurassic era sounds really interesting, Billy, but I'm quite busy at the moment. Can we talk about it after I've finished the ironing?"'

'I did have a lot of ironing that night,' said Mum. 'I have a lot of ironing *every* night.'

'And you said, "Oh, I'd love to know about brontosauruses, but I'm quite busy right now. Let me make the beds first."'

'The beds don't make themselves,' said Mum, yawning a great big yawn.

'And you said, "T-rex is fascinating but he'll have to wait. I'm busy with the hoovering." Mum, you're always busy!'

'I won't deny that,' Mum sighed. 'I

suppose that's why you're in here so early?'

Billy nodded. 'I wanted to catch you when you weren't busy.'

'I *was* busy sleeping,' said Mum, looking longingly at her bed. 'I tell you what. Why don't you leave me one of your dinosaur books? I can learn all about dinosaurs from that.'

'I don't have any dinosaur books,' said Billy, folding his arms and looking pleased with himself. 'I'm an expert on dinosaurs, so I don't need them.'

'Even experts need books,' said Mum. 'Mind you, if you *are* an expert, you could write your own. In fact, you could start right now. Only, close the door on the way out . . .'

Mum snuggled back down into bed.

After a few seconds she sat up again. Billy hadn't budged.

'I can't write a book now,' Billy explained. 'I've got to get ready for school.'

'What about after school?'

Billy shook his head. 'Cartoons are on.'

'Tomorrow night?'

But tomorrow night was swimming. And the next night was Beavers. Then it was football. And the night after that was when Billy slept at Granny and Grandad's. The more Billy thought about it, the more he realised he had no spare time at all.

'You know what it sounds like to me?' said Mum, wriggling back under the covers. 'It sounds like *you're* the one who's too busy!'

But that was about to change . . .

Chapter Two

'Children, I'd like you all to meet Mr Bone,' said Miss Plum during class. 'Mr Bone is a children's writer. He's here to talk about writing. He's offering a prize to the boy or girl who can write the best story: this beautiful illustrated book of dinosaurs!' Miss Plum held the book up for all the children to see.

Billy gazed on excitedly. This was exactly what he needed! With that

book, he could turn Mum into a dinosaur expert in no time. She could catch the odd word while she was ironing. Or scan a paragraph between tucking in beds. Even snatch a sentence while she was hoovering. Why, with that book, they could become a whole family of dinosaur experts!

'Professor Billy, what are you going to call the new dinosaur you've discovered?'

'A Billysaurus.'

'Oh, excellent choice, Professor. And was your discovery a surprise?'

'Nah. I discover new dinosaurs all the time.'

'That's wonderful, Professor. And is it hard work discovering new dinosaurs?'

'Nah. I've got my assistants, Mum and Dad, to do all the digging.'

This was more than a competition. It was the start of a glorious career!

'So, who's going to ask Mr Bone the first question?' asked Miss Plum.

Billy's hand shot up.

'How many words do we have to write?'

Mr Bone shoved his hands deep into his jeans' pockets.

'Dunno. Depends what the words are. Don't want too much rubbish. But you can have too much of a good thing, you know? 'Bout medium, I'd say. Good question, mate.'

Billy beamed.

Beside him, Arty Archie sneered.

'Good question, *not*.'

Billy's heart sank. Right

up until this moment everything had been perfect. Now everything was perfectly horrible. Why couldn't Archie be off sick today? Or be a bit deaf so he couldn't hear Mr Bone? Or have his hand in plaster so he couldn't write? Billy didn't stand a chance against Arty Archie. Arty Archie was brilliant at everything arty.

There was that time the famous painter visited school.

'I painted a picture in watercolours last night, Billy,' Archie had boasted the next day.

'Well, *I* painted a picture using *every* colour, not just the watery ones,' Billy replied.

'You thickhead! You can get every colour in watercolour!'

Then there was the musician who came into assembly.

'Do you play an instrument, Billy?' Archie had asked afterwards. '*I* play the piano.'

'*Everyone* can play the piano,' answered Billy. Everyone except Billy, that was.

'I can play the flute as well,' Archie boasted.

'Well, *I* can play the violin,' Billy answered, not quite

telling the truth.

'The cello,' said Archie, striking back.

'The drums,' Billy fibbed.

'Oboe.'

'Buffoon.'

'Buffoon? You're the buffoon! You mean *bassoon*. The buffoon's not an instrument.'

'You would say that – because *you* can't play it!'

Now here was Mr Bone, the writer. Billy watched miserably as Archie raised his hand. It was going to be the most brilliant question ever asked – Billy could just feel it.

'Mr Bone, which would you prefer,

the first person or the third person?'

Billy perked up. He blinked. Then he blinked again. He shook his head, but no, he wasn't dreaming. Maybe Arty Archie wasn't perfect after all! Of *course* Mr Bone would prefer the first person. The first person had to be the winner, or they wouldn't be the first person!

Billy was surprised by Mr Bone's answer.

'First person. Third person. Both fine by me.'

Mr Bone obviously meant just do your best, Billy thought. First, second or third – it didn't matter which place you came, as long as you tried.

Then Archie's hand was up again.

'Fiction or non-fiction?'

'Don't mind, mate. Either.' Which was fine by Billy, who didn't know the difference anyway.

'Those are all *my* questions,' said Archie when he was finished. He looked at Billy with a snooty expression. 'Now I just need to choose a style. Every great writer has a style. I think I'll choose something unusual. Something sophisticated. Something challenging. Yes, I think I'll write my story in iambic pentameter . . .'

Chapter Three

'Dad, what's Icelandic Perimeter?' Billy asked that evening.

They got out the atlas. There was Iceland. A big white dollop of ice cream floating in icy water.

'A perimeter is something that surrounds something else,' Dad explained.

'But Iceland's surrounded by the sea,' said Billy, peering at the atlas and feeling thoroughly confused.

Dad shrugged. 'Then I guess that's

your Icelandic Perimeter.'

It didn't make sense. Most dinosaurs didn't like water. And none of them liked the cold. So why set a dinosaur story in the freezing cold sea?

Style was all about writing in rhymes. Or putting the words upside down. Or missing out a letter. Like 'e'.

Miss Plum said you couldn't write anything without a letter 'e'. In fact, writing a whole story without a single letter 'e' would take someone really *brilliant* at writing . . .

Billy ran to the cupboard and dragged out paper and pencils. He got scribbling.

Once upon a time . . .

No, no. Remember, *no 'e'*.

Long ago . . .

That was more like it. No 'e', see? This was going to be *so* easy!

Long ago, there lived a dinosaur . . .

No, no. Remember, *no 'e'*.

Long ago was a dinosaur.

Yep. Getting the hang of it.

Long ago was a dinosaur. It was huge . . .

Oops. It couldn't be *huge,* even if it *was* huge.

Long ago was a dinosaur. It was enormous . . .

It couldn't be enormous, either.

It was big . . .

That's it! It was a big dinosaur.

Long ago was a dinosaur. It was big.

Who needed the letter 'e' in the first place?

Long ago was a dinosaur. It was not small. No way. It was big. It was way big. In fact, it was gigantic . . .

Chapter Four

'Ten chapters,' Archie announced the next day.

'*Ten chapters?*' said Billy. His jaw dropped. He gawped at Archie.

Ten chapters was impossible. There wasn't a book in the world that had *ten chapters*.

'It's not much, I know, but it's a start,' said Archie, smiling smugly and pretending to be modest. 'What have *you* managed to write, Billy?'

Billy felt embarrassed. He didn't

even have one chapter, let alone ten. On the other hand, what he did have was *style*.

He took out his little red exercise book and cleared his throat.

'Long ago was a dinosaur. It was not small. No way. It was big. It was way big. In fact, it was gigantic. It had a long tail. It had long hair. It had way big foots. But most of all, it had a gigantic bum . . .'

'You can't write that, it's rude!' said Archie.

'It's not rude,' said Billy. 'Everyone's got a bum. Even the Queen.'

'Not a *gigantic* bum.'

'She would if she didn't have a letter "e".'

'She's got two "e"s,' said Dim David, surprising everyone. 'Q-U-E-N-E.'

'That's not how you spell "queen",' said Billy.

'He's right about the "e"s, though,' Archie pointed out.

'You should use "king" instead,' said

Dim David. 'C–I–N–G.' But everyone ignored him.

'What's wrong with using an "e", anyway?' asked Archie.

Billy thought that would have been obvious to Archie. Archie was the one who'd been going on about style.

'Everyone uses an "e", so I thought I wouldn't,' Billy explained. 'It's my special style.'

A sly grin slithered onto Archie's face. 'It's a special style all right. In fact I think it could be a prize-winner.'

'You do?' said Billy hopefully.

'Yep. If this is the best you can do, you'll win the prize all right. You'll win the prize for *me*!' Archie burst out laughing.

Billy growled and slapped shut his exercise book.

'It's not about taking letters out, it's about putting them in,' said Archie in a hoity-toity voice. 'If you want to be a great writer, you have to use long words . . .'

31

Chapter Five

'Another ten chapters,' Archie announced the next day.

Billy didn't answer.

'Did you hear me, Billy?'

'Hmm?'

'I said, another ten chapters. That makes twenty now.'

'Yeah, whatever.'

'*Twenty* chapters,' Archie repeated.

'Hmm.'

Billy wasn't bothered. It wasn't about the chapters, it was about the words. If Archie wrote a *million* chapters, he wouldn't have words like Billy's. Long words. Posh words. Words that Archie wouldn't even understand. (Some that not even Billy understood, if he was honest.)

'I bet you haven't written a single chapter,' said Archie spitefully.

Billy didn't answer. He sighed a bored sigh.

'I bet you haven't even written a single *word*!'

Billy gave a big bored shrug. He opened his little red exercise book and gave a big bored yawn. Then he began to read in a bored voice.

'Once upon a time there was a creature of the dinosaur species. He possessed two companions. On one occasion, they embarked upon a picnic. They searched for a location

to sit.

'Where are we going to sit?" asked the first dinosaur.

The second dinosaur said, "I've got a spot."

"On my bottom!" said the third dinosaur to the first dinosaur.'

Archie snatched Billy's book off him.

'Give it back!' growled Billy.

Billy lunged for it, but Archie hugged it to himself.

'Blah, blah blah,' Archie muttered, skipping through the words. Then he stopped. And started to grin. And read out in a loud voice, 'I've got a spot on my bottom!'

Miss Plum overheard.

'Archie, I won't have that language in class!'

'It's not me, Miss. It's Billy. He's the

one with the spot on his bottom!'

'You're reading it the wrong way!' hissed Billy.

'I'm reading it the way *you* wrote it,' said Archie.

By now the whole class was laughing and pointing at Billy.

'Billy's got a spot on his bot-tom! Billy's got a spot on his bot-tom!'

'Now look what you've done!' said Billy.

Archie shrugged. 'It shows you're turning into a true writer.'

'Now you're teasing me!' Billy wasn't sounding bored any more. All his cool had evaporated. 'Why are you being so horrible?'

'Me? Your one true friend?'

'You're not my friend!'

'I'm your *only* friend at the moment, Billy. See how the others are making fun of you? That's what happens to great writers.'

Billy didn't answer. He folded his arms and glared at Archie furiously. He didn't want to believe him. But the rest of the class certainly *were* making fun of him. He thought writing a dinosaur story would be easy. He hadn't expected the whole class to start making fun of him.

'True writers always have people making fun of them,' explained Archie, as if this were something everyone knew. 'That's why you don't see many true writers. They hide away. A truly great writer does his work at night, when everyone else is asleep. Oh, yes, if you want to be a great writer, you have to stay up late . . .'

Chapter Six

'I think I'll go straight up to bed,' said Billy after dinner.

Mum dropped her fork.

Dad nearly choked.

'Are you tired, sweetheart?' asked Mum, frowning her 'You're ill' frown. 'Tiredness can mean all sorts of things.'

'Nah. I just think a good night's sleep is important.'

Dad was suspicious. 'What are you planning, Billy?'

Billy's reply was as innocent as

anything. 'I'm planning to get a good night's rest, that's all. Night night.'

If staying up was what it took to write a great story, Billy was going to write a masterpiece! He was the King of Staying Up.

At Uncle David's wedding, he stayed up till the disco started.

On holiday once, he stayed up till the stars came out.

And at bedtime, no child in the world could stay up like he could – so Mum said.

He'd have a nap now, then when everyone was asleep, he'd get up again.

Except – he thought as he lay down on his bed – what if he didn't wake up till morning? No masterpiece. And Archie would have written another ten chapters! Napping was too big a risk.

So Billy got up. There was nothing

else for it but to stay awake all night.

That proved hard even for the King of Staying Up.

Billy started feeling sleepy in no time at all. Nothing he tried would make the feeling go away.

He tried walking around his room.

He tried splashing water on his face.

He tried sellotaping his eyelids open.

Billy tried everything, but nothing worked.

Which is why when the last light went off downstairs, Billy was already fast asleep.

Chapter Seven

'Another ten chapters,' Archie announced the next day. 'That's thirty chapters, now.'

'Unagh,' grunted Billy, his eyes closed.

'What was that?'

'Umum.'

'I hope that's not the title of your story! Ha ha! Ha ha ha!'

'Grumuma,' mumbled Billy, too tired to argue.

Billy sat slumped at his desk, his

head resting on his arms. Underneath his left elbow lay his little red exercise book.

Archie spotted it and snatched it away.

'So this is your great masterpiece,' he sneered. He peeled the pages open one by one. Every line on every page was crossed out. Only one line was left – on the very last page. Archie read it out loud.

'Once upon a time there was a dinosaur.'

'Not very long, is it?' said Archie.

'Isqualidynodquandidy.'

'Who's talking in class?' Miss Plum called out.

The whole class went suddenly quiet. Silence everywhere.

Except for a little spot right near Billy.

'Isqualidynodquandidy.'

He was still mumbling when Mum arrived to take him out of school.

'Isqualidynodquandidy . . . Isqualidynodquandidy . . .'

'You see what I mean?' said Miss Plum worriedly. 'He's just talking nonsense.'

'He's always talking nonsense,' said Mum. 'But he's never normally this tired. He even went to bed early last night. I'd better get him home.'

Chapter Eight

'Falling asleep in class,' said Mum, folding her arms and fixing Billy with a fierce look. 'And Miss Plum says you haven't been writing your story.'

'I *have* been writing it! I'm just a bit stuck, that's all.'

Mum narrowed her eyes suspiciously. This sounded like an excuse. Billy was brilliant at excuses.

'Which bit are you stuck on?'

'Well, the beginning's a bit difficult.'

'What else?'

'The middle,' said Billy. 'I can't decide about the middle.'

'Well, you can decide about that nearer the time. What about the end?'

'I've got lots of ends. But I can't decide which one to use.'

If this was an excuse, it was a convincing one, thought Mum. Billy was thoroughly down in the dumps.

'You know what I think is wrong?' said Mum. 'I think you've got writer's block. That's when you've got so many ideas in your head, they won't come out.'

That was it! It wasn't because he was *no* good. It was

because he was *too* good! All those
ideas, like sweets in a jar. All jammed
in. Well that was easily remedied.

Billy stood up. Then he jumped.
Then he jumped again. And jumped
and jumped and shook and shook and
shook his head. He managed a full ten
seconds before keeling over onto his
bed.

There he lay with the
room spinning and
his head hurting.
'Feel   any
better for that?'
asked   Mum,
trying   not   to
laugh.

'Not   really.
My head hurts.'
'I'm   not
surprised.'

'And it still feels blocked.'

'Maybe you're trying too hard,' said Mum.

'But I have to try hard,' said Billy. 'I want to be the first person.'

Then he could win that book and Mum could learn about dinosaurs. Then she and Dad could dig him a big hole and he could discover a Billysaurus.

Mum smiled. 'Don't try to be the best. Just try to be yourself. Be natural. Write what comes to you naturally, and you never know, you might turn out to be the best anyway.'

Billy thought about that. It wasn't easy when your head was spinning, but he thought about it. Mum *might* be right. Maybe it *would* work if he was natural. After all, he *was* a natural when it came to writing. But something about Mum's plan was still bothering him.

'What if I'm being myself and I *still* get stuck?'

Mum shrugged. 'Well, you could always ask for help.'

Billy sat up sharply. 'I don't need help! I'm an expert!'

'I'm sure you are, sweetheart, but even experts need help sometimes.'

That was news to Billy. He'd never heard of it. Experts knew everything. What help could an expert possibly need?

'How do you think experts get to *be* experts in the first place?' said Mum. 'It's only by asking questions.'

'But I'm the world's expert on dinosaurs and writing,' said Billy. 'There's nobody who knows more about dinosaurs and writing than me.'

Mum smiled. 'Getting help doesn't only mean getting answers. Sometimes the answers are inside you already. You just need someone to help you find them.'

'But who can I ask?'

'Well, that depends on the question,' said Mum. 'What's the one, single thing you're most stuck on with this story of yours?'

'The words,' said Billy glumly. 'I don't know what words to put.'

Mum shrugged. 'Then that's your question.'

Chapter Nine

Billy decided to write a letter to Mr Bone. Mr Bone was the nearest thing Billy knew to an expert (besides himself, of course). He wrote:

Dear Mr. Bone,

I don't know what words to put.

From Billy

He got a reply the very next day:

Billy, mate,
   If it's words you want,
find a thesaurus.
   A thesaurus is, like,
well good for words.
            From Mr. Bone

A thesaurus? Billy knew every kind of dinosaur, but he'd never heard of a *thesaurus*.

It must be a secret. Only government scientists knew. And secret agents. And the prime minister. It was a conspiracy! But why keep a dinosaur secret?

Because it was *unlike any other dinosaur*.

Why, if people even *saw* a thesaurus, there'd be riots in the streets!

It had eighteen legs and five wings.

No, it had eyes on stalks.

No, it had an invisible body but arms and legs you could see.

It was *alive*!

A living dinosaur! What a story that would make! Oh, thank you, Mr Bone!

TO: Prime Minister
FROM: Ministry of Defence
SUBJECT: THESAURUS

TOP SECRET

TOP SECRET

TOP SECRET

STATUS: Active

Invisible body

Fig. 1 Artist's Impression

TOP SECRET

Recent sightings:
- Hyde Park (large droppings found)
- Downing Street (unconfirmed, suspicious smell)
- Dinosaur Museum (confirmed by Dinosaur Experts)
- Wembley Stadium (match disrupted)
- Paddington Station (possible sighting Platform 13, many reports of loud snuffling noises) (drinking from

Chapter Ten

'Right, then, what's it to be?' asked Dad on Saturday morning. 'Swimming? Ice-skating? We could go bowling. We haven't done that for a while.'

'The dinosaur museum,' said Billy.

'A load of dusty old dinosaur bones? What about a stroll through the park?'

'The dinosaur museum.'

'I know! A film. Sit in the cinema. Munch some popcorn. We could all go.'

'I'm far too busy,' said Mum.

'Just you and me then, Billy,' said Dad. 'The cinema. What do you say?'

'The dinosaur museum.'

So the dinosaur museum it was, and the hunt for the thesaurus.

Chapter Eleven

The dinosaur museum was full of skeletons. Billy strolled past one after another, scanning the labels.

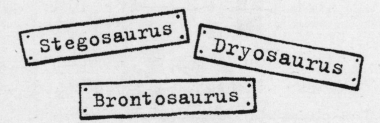

Wow. Brontosauruses were *big*. Billy walked on.

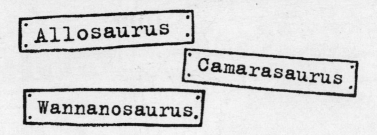

No shortage of sauruses, but no thesaurus. Billy kept on walking.

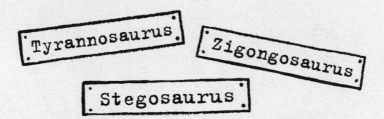

Hold on. Hadn't he seen a stegosaurus already? He must have taken a wrong turn. Now he'd have to start all over again.

This time he was going to write down the dinosaur names so he wouldn't get mixed up.

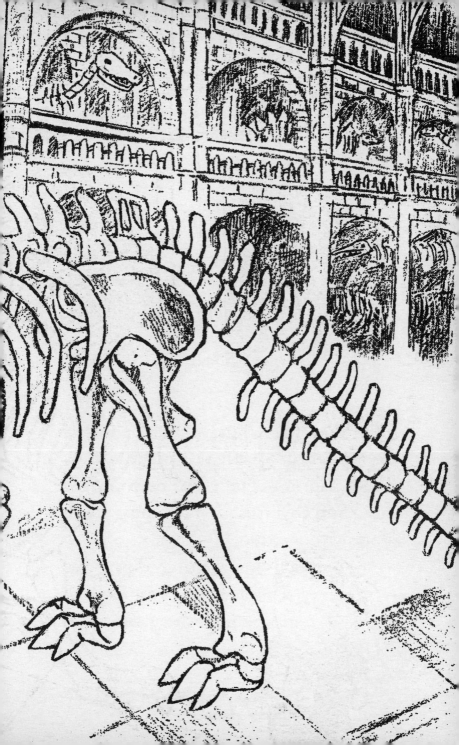

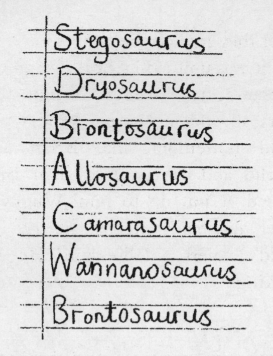

Stegosaurus
Dryosaurus
Brontosaurus
Allosaurus
Camarasaurus
Wannanosaurus
Brontosaurus

Hold on. That was another brontosaurus. That made two brontosauruses. There was no room for *two* brontosauruses! He must have gone wrong again.

So much for writing down the names. Dinosaur names didn't all just sound the same – on paper they looked the same, too.

If it was up to Billy, he'd give all the dinosaurs new names. Names that didn't all end in 'saurus'. Names you could remember, like Brian and Charlie and Trevor. And then Billy realised: it *was* up to him! Who was better qualified? After all, he *was* the world's expert on dinosaurs! He got thinking.

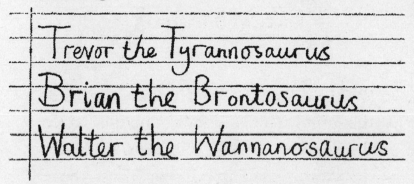

Trevor the Tyrannosaurus
Brian the Brontosaurus
Walter the Wannanosaurus

It was getting easier to remember them already. They weren't just dry old bones any more. They were turning into real characters.

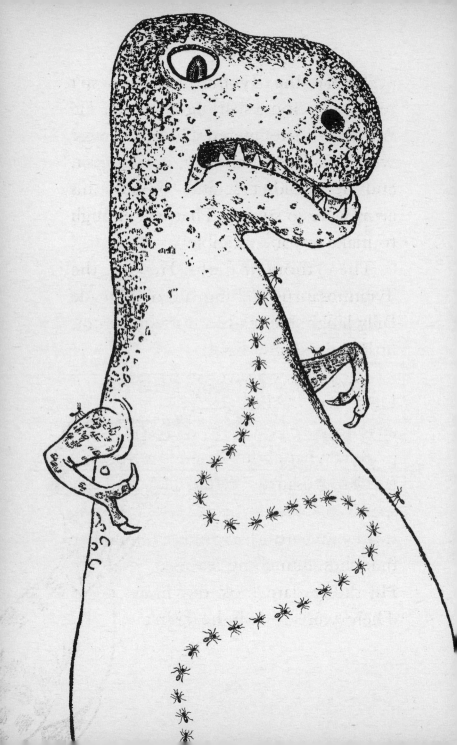

Trevor the Tyrannosaurus wasn't really a vicious, snarling monster. He was just bad-tempered. He had trouble with ants. They made him itch all over, and he couldn't scratch because his arms were so stumpy. That was enough to make anyone irritable!

The thought of Trevor the Tyrannosaurus itching all over made Billy laugh. He made a note of it in his little red exercise book.

Allosaurus was ever so friendly. He'd say 'Allo' to 'Allo anyone!

And what about Brian the Brontosaurus? Brian spent all day with his head up in the high branches, munching leaves. He didn't dare look down. There were . . . oh, he didn't

even dare say it . . . there
were *mice* on the ground!
Brian was bigger than a hundred
houses, but mice sent him into a
    quiver!

Billy laughed and wrote it down. Then there was Walter the Wannanosaurus. He was so nosy. He was into everything. Whatever was going on, Walter the Wannanosaurus wanted to know.

Billy wrote it down.

He was so busy writing, it was getting so he couldn't stop.

Dryosaurus never went in the water.
He preferred being dryo.

Camarasaurus was always taking photos.

Scribble, scribble, scribble.
Billy had his head so deep in his

exercise book he didn't notice Mr
Bone. He walked straight into him.

'Hi there, Billy, mate,' said Mr Bone,
as if people walked into him all the
time. 'Doing some research?'

Billy looked up at Mr Bone. 'I'm
searching for a dinosaur.'

'Me too. Dinosaur museum. Best
place to look. Tell you what, though.
Been here a hundred times, and can I
remember the names? Not likely!'

'I've been writing them down,'
said Billy.

'Cool.'

Billy knew he must be getting close
to the thesaurus. Mr Bone would be
looking for it too, and here was Mr
Bone right in front of him. That meant
the thesaurus couldn't be far away. Billy
peered round Mr Bone at the endless

rows of skeletons.

'Lost something, mate?' asked Mr Bone.

'I can't find my thesaurus.'

'Stuff's always going walkabout in here.'

Billy's eyes nearly popped out of his head. He dropped his little red exercise book. 'You mean it actually *walks about*?'

Billy wanted so hard to find the thesaurus, he hadn't thought about the thesaurus finding him! What if it were a vicious predator like *tyrannosaurus rex*?

'Don't worry about your thesaurus, mate,' said Mr Bone. 'Somebody'll find it and hand it in.'

But Billy was already dashing for the door.

Chapter Twelve

'How's the story coming on?' asked Mum, coming into Billy's bedroom.

'I still don't know what words to put,' said Billy, lying on his bed and feeling miserable. 'Not that it matters now, anyway. It's too late.'

The competition was over. Archie would have won. Archie would have the book and he'd grow up to be an expert on dinosaurs. No Billysaurus. It would be an Archiesaurus instead. And all because the thesaurus went walkabout. Billy was beginning to hate sauruses.

'I've got some visitors here who might cheer you up,' said Mum.

Mr Bone and Miss Plum came in.

'Found something of yours, mate,' said Mr Bone.

Billy sat up eagerly. *The thesaurus!*

'Has it got eighteen legs and five wings?'

Mr Bone smiled and shook his head. 'Boy, the books I could write if I had your imagination, Billy. No, it hasn't got legs or wings. But it does have leaves and a spine.'

That was even stranger than Billy had imagined.

'Does it have eyes on stalks?'

Mr Bone shook his head. 'The "i"s are inside.'

'Yuk. And is it . . . invisible?'

'It was until I found it,' said Mr Bone, laughing. 'I thought you might need it, so I brought it with me.'

'You brought it *with you*?' gulped Billy, not sure he wanted to meet a thesaurus face to face.

But it wasn't a thesaurus. It wasn't any kind of dinosaur. It was just his little red exercise book. Billy's face fell.

'You dropped it on the museum

floor,' said Mr Bone.

'You should have left it there,' said Billy miserably. 'There's nothing in it worth keeping.'

Mr Bone looked surprised. 'Hey, Billy, mate, you're joking, right? I mean, Trevor the T-rex, bothered by ants, can't scratch 'cause his arms are too short. Brian the Brontosaurus, scared of mice. Walter the Wannanosaurus, "I wanna know!" I tell you, I nearly fell out of my chair with laughter. But I learnt loads at the same time. Best thing I've read in years.'

Billy looked up. Mr Bone was smiling. Miss Plum was smiling. Mum was smiling. They couldn't all be smiling for nothing. Was it possible he'd won the prize after all?

'I haven't . . . I mean, I didn't . . . I mean, have I . . . ?'

Miss Plum patted Billy's hand.

'I'm sorry, Billy. The prize for the best story went to someone else.'

'Bet it was Archie,' said Billy.

Miss Plum looked surprised. 'Archie? Oh, no, it wasn't Archie.'

'But Archie's brilliant at writing!' said Billy.

'Archie *thinks* he's brilliant at writing,' said Miss Plum. 'No, the prize went to David.'

'Not Dim David!'

'Not *dim* David at all,' said Miss Plum. 'David's story was very clever. And funny. It was about a dinosaur with a big bottom . . .'

'Yeah. Short and sweet,' said Mr Bone. 'I mean, the story, not the kid.'

'I don't think David even thought about winning,' said Miss Plum. 'He just did his best. Doing your best is the best thing you *can* do.'

'I was going to win Mr Bone's dinosaur book and give it to Mum,' said Billy sadly. 'Then she could learn all about dinosaurs.'

Mum smiled at Billy. 'I don't need Mr Bone's dinosaur book. I'm going to wait until *your* dinosaur book comes out.'

'But I don't have a dinosaur book,' said Billy, puzzled.

'You will have,' said Miss Plum, grinning.

'Yeah,' said Mr Bone. He picked up Billy's little red exercise book. 'I want to take this to my publisher. Publish it. Turn it into a proper book. A book with *your* name on the front.'

'Publish it?' croaked Billy.

'You've got it, mate. Oh, and one more thing. Here.' Mr Bone tossed a different book onto Billy's bed. 'Keep on writing, mate.'

Billy looked at the book on his bed. Printed on the cover was a single word.

'That's not a fierce predator that's going to bite me,' said Billy quietly.

Mr Bone laughed. 'That's what I tell you kids all the time. "Writing doesn't bite".'

'It hasn't even got any teeth.'

Mr Bone laughed and shook his head. 'Billy, you crack me up.'

'I thought a thesaurus was a dinosaur,' said Billy. Mr Bone roared with laughter.

'A thesaurus is a book a bit like a dictionary,' explained Miss Plum. 'It tells you words that are like other words. For example, you might be happy, but you want a different word for it . . .'

'So look in the thesaurus—' said Mr Bone.

'And you'll find other words,' said Miss Plum.

'Yeah, like: Billy's pleased; Billy's content; Billy's jubilant; Billy's ecstatic.' Billy was all of those things.